The STRANGE WEINER DOG and ME

Dr. B. B. Hightower

Archway Publishing books may be ordered through booksellers or by contacting:

Archway Publishing
1663 Liberty Drive
Bloomington, IN 47403
www.archwaypublishing.com
1 (888) 242-5904

ISBN: 978-1-4808-8564-6 (sc)
ISBN: 978-1-4808-8565-3 (hc)
ISBN: 978-1-4808-8566-0 (e)

Print information available on the last page.

Archway Publishing rev. date: 12/6/2019

The
Strange Weiner Dog & Me

Written by: Dr. B.B. Hightower

I saw a strange weiner dog;

he was sitting in a tree...

I looked up and laughed, and he laughed right back at me...

I didn't like that, not one bit
at all, so I shook the tree a bit
and I watched him fall...

He fell from the tree, down
into some plants...

Then he chased me down, and

bit a hole in my pants....

As I ran, I tripped and fell hard on the ground... And then the strange weiner dog, this different little hound...

Licked my sad face...

And snuggled against my neck...

So, I put my arms around him,

and gave him a little peck...

We walked home together, and
guess how this story ends...

The strange weiner dog and

I, became best friends...

DR. B. B. HIGHTOWER is an educator who has taught in a variety of educational settings. He is currently an adjunct professor instructing aspiring teachers. He and his wife enjoy spending time with their family, friends, and pets.